Prayers and Poems

Contributing Writer: Marlene Targ Brill

Consultant: David M. Howard, Jr., Ph.D.

Cover Illustration: Stephen Marchesi

Book Illustrations: Thomas Gianni

David M. Howard, Jr., Ph.D. is an associate professor of Old Testament
and Semitic Languages, and is a member of the Society of Biblical
Literature and the Institute for Biblical Research.

The publisher has made every effort to verify the accuracy of the material
in this book and to obtain permission to reprint, where necessary. Any
errors are unintentional, and corrections will be made in future editions if
necessary.

Thank you for the world
so sweet,
Thank you for the food
we eat,
Thank you for the birds
that sing,
Thank you, God,
for everything!

Lord teach a little child to pray
And then accept my prayer,
Thou hearest all the words I say
For Thou art everywhere.

God is great,
God is good.
Let us thank Him
for our food. Amen.

Blessed are You, Oh Lord our God, King of all the world, Who makes bread grow from the earth.

Bless us, Oh Lord,
For these Thy gifts,
Which we are about to receive
From Thy bounty.
Through Christ our Lord. Amen.

God be in my head,
And in my understanding;
God be in my eyes,
And in my looking;

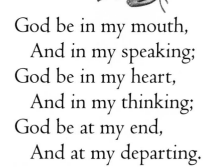

God be in my mouth,
And in my speaking;
God be in my heart,
And in my thinking;
God be at my end,
And at my departing.

To do to others as I would
That they should do to me,
Will make me gentle, kind, and good,
As children ought to be.

God made the sun
    And God made the trees,
God made the mountains
    And God made me.

I thank you, O God,
    For the sun and the trees,
For making the mountains
    And for making me.

I see the moon,
    And the moon sees me.
God bless the moon,
    And God bless me.

All things bright and beautiful,
  All creatures great and small,
All things wise and wonderful,
  The Lord God made them all.

        Each little flower that opens,
          Each little bird that sings,
        He made their glowing colors,
          He made their tiny wings.

The tall trees in the greenwood,
  The meadows where we play,
The rushes by the water,
  We gather every day—

        He gave us eyes to see them,
          And lips that we might tell
        How great is God Almighty,
          Who has made all things well!

Two little eyes to look to God;
 Two little ears to hear His word;
 Two little feet to walk in His ways;
 Hands to serve Him all my days.

What can I give Him,
 Poor as I am?
If I were a shepherd,
 I would bring a lamb.
If I were a Wise Man,
 I would do my part.
But what can I give Him—
 Give Him my heart.

Jesus, friend of little children,
    Be a friend to me
  Take my hand and ever keep me
    Close to thee.

      Teach me how to grow in goodness,
        Daily as I grow;
      Thou hast been a child, and surely
        Thou dost know.

           Never leave me, nor forsake me;
             Ever be my friend;
           For I need thee, from life's dawning
             To its end.

Sleep, my child, and peace attend thee,
   All through the night;
Guardian angels God will send thee,
   All through the night;

      Soft the drowsy hours are creeping,
         Hill and vale in slumber sleeping,
      I my loving vigil keeping,
         All through the night.

While the moon her watch is keeping,
   All through the night;
While the weary world is sleeping,
   All through the night;

      O'er thy spirit gently stealing,
         Visions of delight revealing,
      Breathes a pure and holy feeling,
         All through the night.

Our Father,
Who art in heaven,
Hallowed be Thy name.
Thy kingdom come,
Thy will be done,
On earth as it is in heaven.
Give us this day our daily bread,
And forgive us our trespasses,
As we forgive others who trespass against us.
Lead us not into temptation,
But deliver us from evil;
For Thine is the kingdom,
And the power,
And the glory,
Forever and ever. Amen.

Day is done,
    Gone the sun,
    From the lake,
    From the hills,
    From the sky.
    All is well,
    Safely rest,
    God is nigh.

May the Lord bless you and keep you.
    May the Lord make His face shine upon you and
        be gracious to you.
    May the Lord turn His face toward you and give
        you peace.